BAT
and the Waiting Game

Also by Elana K. Arnold
A Boy Called Bat

BAT
and the Waiting Game

WRITTEN BY

Elana K. Arnold

WITH PICTURES BY

Charles Santoso

WALDEN POND PRESS™

An Imprint of HarperCollins*Publishers*

Walden Pond Press is an imprint of HarperCollins Publishers.
Walden Pond Press and the skipping stone logo are trademarks and
registered trademarks of Walden Media, LLC.

Bat and the Waiting Game
Text copyright © 2018 by Elana K. Arnold
Illustrations copyright © 2018 by Charles Santoso

Library of Congress Control Number: 2017934990
ISBN 978-0-06-244585-8

Typography by Aurora Parlagreco
18 19 20 21 22   CG/LSCH   10 9 8 7 6 5 4 3 2 1

First Edition

For Davis, our Star

Contents

BAT
and the Waiting Game

CHAPTER 1
Skunk Kits

Maybe, Bat thought, there was something better in the world than cradling a sleepy, just-fed baby skunk in your arms. But at this moment, it didn't seem likely.

Bat was sitting in his beanbag chair, having just put down the tiny, nearly empty bottle of formula. In Bat's hand, licking his fine soft whiskers with a tiny pink tongue and then yawning widely to reveal two rows of new white teeth, was a six-week-old skunk kit named Thor.

After licking his whiskers clean, Thor curled up into a ball in Bat's hand, and Bat held the tiny creature close to his chest, carefully settling into his beanbag, watching as Thor fell into contented sleep.

It had been one week since Bat's mother had agreed that the family could continue caring for the skunk kit until he was old enough to be released into the wild, and Bat could still barely believe his good luck.

With the soft, warm weight of Thor in his hands, Bat looked around his room. He sat across from his window, the bamboo shade rolled all the way up. The window was half open, and a pleasant breeze blew in. It was springtime, and the air was beginning to feel warm.

Bat's bed was neatly made just the way he liked it, with the blue sheet and red-and-blue-plaid quilt tucked in tight so that when he climbed in at night he would feel like he was slipping into a cocoon. A matching red-and-blue-plaid quilt peeked out from the trundle underneath Bat's bed.

There was the honey-brown dresser where Bat kept his clothes neatly sorted just how he liked them, and beside it was Bat's bookshelf, where he kept all his important things, including his favorite possession, his animal encyclopedia. And there, right next to the animal encyclopedia, was something new.

From where Bat sat, the new thing looked like an oddly shaped lump of clay, but Bat had spent enough time holding it and examining it from all angles to know that it was actually art.

It was a sculpture of a skunk kit, molded out

of gray clay, with eyes and a nose and a mouth carved into it and, on the bottom, the words "From Israel" carved in, too.

When Israel had first handed it to Bat last Monday at school, it had taken Bat a moment to figure out what exactly he was holding.

"It's a skunk kit!" Israel said. "I made it in my mom's studio. She fired it in her kiln and everything. So this way, when you're not at home with Thor, you can still have a skunk with you. You know, you can carry it around! Like, in your pocket or something."

Bat had rubbed his thumb down the smooth shiny back of the clay lump. It didn't look much like a skunk kit, but its pleasant weight felt good in his hand. And when he had flipped it over to find the words "From Israel" on the bottom, a warm good feeling spread through his chest and up his neck.

A friend had given him a gift. And even if it didn't look much like the real baby skunk now nestled in his hands, it definitely deserved a place on his bookshelf, along with his other important things.

CHAPTER 2
Dinner Conversation

Setting the table for dinner was one of Bat's jobs, but that evening, placing three plates, three cups, and three forks on three placemats, he felt very certain that his sister, Janie, should have this job instead.

For one thing, she refused to let Bat carry Thor while he set the table.

"He's tucked into his sling, Janie," Bat argued.

Laurence, the veterinary technician who worked with Mom, had made the sling so that Bat could safely carry Thor around. "He's not anywhere *near* your plate and fork and cup!"

Janie just shook her head and crossed her arms. "It's not sanitary," she said. "You'd be violating like three different health code regulations."

Her logic wasn't logical, but Bat screwed his mouth up tight and breathed in deeply through his nose. One of Mom's conditions for raising the skunk kit was "No family disharmony." Which meant that Bat wasn't supposed to be stubborn about skunk stuff like setting the table with the skunk in his sling. So he turned around and headed back to his room, where he lifted the sling from where it hung around his neck and tucked it, sleeping Thor still inside, into the enclosure, a repurposed dog crate. At least Mom had finally

agreed to let Thor sleep in Bat's room. That was
something.

He didn't *mean* to slam the dishes down on the
table. Not *really*. And probably Janie wouldn't even
notice that he put her fork upside down instead of
right side up.

But she *did* notice, a few minutes later, when
Bat filled Mom's cup and his own cup with lemon-
ade and Janie's cup with plain water.

"Thank you, Bat," she said with a big smile. "Sugar isn't good for my voice before an important audition." And then she took a big gulp of the water like it was the best thing she had ever tasted.

"Are you nervous?" Mom asked, spooning enchiladas onto each of the three plates. The hot melted cheese stretched into long strings as the enchiladas traveled from the serving dish to the plates.

"No," said Janie. "Well, maybe a little."

Bat waited for Mom to cut his enchilada into pieces. He liked the taste of enchiladas, but the texture of the cheese sometimes grossed him out a little. It was better if Mom cut it into little cubes for him.

"Bat, aren't you old enough to cut your own food?" Janie asked.

"Yes," Bat answered. "But Mom does it better."

"Well, you'll never get good at it unless you practice," Janie said. Bat didn't like the tone of her voice—kind of like a know-it-all.

"Sometimes even practicing at something doesn't mean you'll ever get good at it," he said. "Like you and singing."

"Bat," Mom said, in her low warning voice.

Bat shrugged. If Janie was going to be mean, he could be mean, too, even though he secretly thought that Janie had a beautiful singing voice.

They were quiet for a few minutes, just their forks scraping plates and the clink of their cups being set back down.

"So you're set on auditioning for the queen?" Mom asked.

Janie nodded. "It's the best part," she said. "There's the most room for artistic creativity."

Janie had been talking about auditioning for

her school's spring play for weeks now. They were going to perform *Alice in Wonderland* during the last week of school, and the audition was in just a few days.

"I'm glad the audition is on Monday," Bat said, stabbing an enchilada cube with his fork.

Mom smiled. "That's nice of you, Bat."

"Then Janie can stop talking about it all the time." Bat popped the enchilada cube into his mouth. Delicious.

"I don't talk about the audition nearly as much as you talk about Thor," Janie said.

"How much can anyone say about an audition?" Bat said.

"How much can anyone say about a *skunk*?" Janie said.

"Well," said Bat, "did you know that skunks sometimes attack beehives because they like to eat honeybees? And that a wild skunk usually only lives about three years, but pet skunks can live up to ten? Or how about this—skunks can survive a snakebite! And skunks aren't fast. And they have bad eyesight. And—"

Bat had a lot more he could have said, but Mom interrupted. "How about this," she said. "What do the two of you have to say about dessert?"

Dessert was something that was easy to agree on, Bat thought happily as Mom served him one of the still-warm brownies that Janie had made that afternoon.

CHAPTER 3
Parts

The next day was Saturday, and since it wasn't an Every-Other Weekend, Bat got to spend the whole day with Thor.

On Every-Other Weekends, Dad picked Bat and Janie up when school was finished on Friday and took them home to his apartment. There were good things about Every-Other Weekends: Dad liked to go on bike rides; Dad had a small garage, which he kept neatly organized, and it was a good place to build things; there was a workout room at Dad's apartment complex that Bat wasn't old enough to use yet, but would be, one day.

But especially since Thor had joined the family, Bat wasn't really a fan of Every-Other Weekends, because Dad wasn't a fan of animals. Mom, on the other hand, was almost as crazy about animals as Bat was.

In lots of ways, Mom and Dad were opposites: Mom liked animals; Dad didn't. Mom worked as a veterinarian; Dad worked as a computer engineer. Mom liked to stay at home on the weekends, reading books and gardening; Dad liked to go out into the world on weekends, bike riding and playing catch at the park.

Bat liked animals, and he liked computers, too. He liked to stay home, and he liked to go out into the world. And his name was even made up of parts of both of his parents' names: Bat was short for Bixby Alexander Tam—"Bixby" from his mom's last name when she was a kid, "Alexander" because that was his dad's middle name.

Bat liked that he had parts of both of his parents' names in his name. It made sense, since he had parts of both of his parents in the rest of him, too. He had his dad's straight black hair, which came from his dad's Chinese ancestry, and he had his mom's long fingers. He had his mom's love of chocolate and his dad's aversion to touching yucky things.

When Bat woke up on Saturday, the first thing he did after going to the bathroom and washing his hands was scoop Thor out of his enclosure and tuck him into the sling. Thor was getting bigger, Bat thought with satisfaction. His little belly had started to round out from all the formula Bat had been feeding him. Bat was a good skunk caretaker.

The kitchen was quiet; Mom and Janie were still asleep. Carefully, Bat poured a kit-sized serving of formula into Thor's tiny bottle. He screwed the lid on tightly and then held the bottle under warm running water so the formula wouldn't be cold.

It was a beautiful day, Bat saw through the window above the kitchen sink. The leaves on the tree were quiet—no wind—and the sky was a clear bright blue, with just a little bit of violet still from sunrise.

"Would you like to dine *al fresco*?" Bat said to Thor. *Al fresco* was Italian for "outside," Bat knew, because on sunny days at school, his teacher, Mr. Grayson, sometimes said, "Hey, gang, let's do reading time *al fresco*."

Bat took the bottle and went out through the

back door, sitting on the brick steps that led down into the yard. Thor must have smelled breakfast, because he was rustling around in the sling. Gently, Bat scooped him out and settled him on his lap.

Six weeks ago, when Thor had just been born, his nose had been pink, but now it was darkening to a nice shiny black. It twitched up at the bottle, and Bat aimed the bottle down. Thor's tongue darted out and soon he was happily lapping up the formula, drop by drop.

Bat liked it when he could concentrate on just one thing, and he liked it even better when the one thing he was concentrating on was something he loved, like taking care of Thor.

With his thumb, Bat gently stroked the white strip of fur that ran up Thor's snout and over his head. Thor closed his shiny black eyes and it looked to Bat like he grinned, short milky whisker hairs curving upward.

The back door opened and Bat turned to see Janie standing in the doorway. Her hair, which was not quite as dark as Bat's, was wrapped around a bunch of spongy pink curlers.

"Hey," said Janie.

"Hey," said Bat.

Janie came the rest of the way outside and sat down on the step next to Bat, peering down at Thor. "He's getting cuter," she said.

"He's getting furrier," said Bat, "but I think he's always been all the way cute."

Janie made a noise halfway between a grunt and a snort. Then she said, "When is he going to start spraying?"

"That depends," Bat said. He set down the empty bottle and tucked Thor back into the sling.

"Skunks only spray if they feel threatened. If Thor never feels threatened, maybe he'll never spray."

"I guess you'll have to try really hard to stay calm, huh?" said Janie. "Even if I tease you or tickle you?" She lifted up her hands and wiggled her fingers.

Bat hated to be tickled. "Don't," he said, but he tried to say it in a really calm voice because he didn't want to make Thor nervous.

Janie laughed. "Just kidding, Bat," she said. "Hey, do you want to help me take the curlers out of my hair?"

Bat liked to help Janie with hair stuff, and she barely ever let him. "Okay," he answered. "Just let me put Thor away first."

CHAPTER 4
A Stinky Joke

After breakfast, Ezra came over to help Janie practice for her big audition. Janie thought Ezra was *hilarious*, but usually Bat did not agree.

"Hey, Batty," Ezra said when he arrived. "I've got a joke for you. Okay. What do you call a flying skunk?"

"Actually," Bat said, "skunks can't fly. They're mammals, and the only flying mammal is the—"

"A *smell*icopter!" Ezra interrupted. Then he laughed, loudly, at his own joke.

There were so many things wrong with the whole situation that Bat felt himself starting to rise up on his toes the way he sometimes did, and pulling his arms close to his sides the way he sometimes did, hands preparing to flap.

Ezra laughed even louder. "Hey!" he said. "*You're* the flying mammal, right? Because you're Bat! Good one, Batty."

"Come *on*, Ezra," Janie said, and Ezra followed her out of the entry hall and toward the kitchen, still laughing.

When the hallway was quiet, Bat remembered to take deep breaths and he let himself bounce on the balls of his feet ten more times before putting his heels on the floor. He wiggled his shoulders around the way that helped him relax, and his arms dropped slowly to his sides.

"Little Bat," crooned Mom from behind him. "Are you all right?"

Bat nodded. He didn't feel like talking. Mom came around to his front and held out her arms. She knew that Bat sometimes didn't feel like being touched when he was upset, and this was her way of letting him know that she was there if he wanted a hug. All he had to do was take one step forward, which, after a moment's hesitation, he did.

Mom pulled him close, and Bat closed his eyes as he let his face mush into the softness of her stomach. He felt the snug tightness of her arms around his shoulders and back, the gentle firm pressure of her embrace. He felt safe and warm and let himself take a long, deep breath.

Mom smelled of rosemary, like sunshine and peppermint and pine. Bat took another deep breath before he tapped his hand against Mom's leg, their sign that he was ready for the hug to be over.

She loosened her arms and stepped back.

"Are you gardening?" Bat asked.

"Yes," Mom said. "Do you want to help?"

"Yes," said Bat, and then he had a really good idea. "Mom," he said. "Do you think we could research what kind of vegetables skunks like to eat and plant them in the garden box in the backyard?" He looked up at Mom's face, excited.

"I think that's a great idea," Mom said. "A research project! And maybe you could ask Israel if he'd like to help."

And then Bat had another idea. "We have to do a spring project for school," he said. "And we're supposed to have a partner. Maybe Israel's and my project could be researching and growing a skunk garden!"

"You'd better not plant any roses," said Ezra. He and Janie had just walked back into the hallway on their way to the front yard. "Get it? Because roses smell *good*!"

"Oh, Ezra," Mom said. "That joke really stinks."

That time, everyone, even Bat, laughed.

CHAPTER 5
Almost Late

On Monday, Bat waited outside of the school for Israel to arrive. Mom waited with him.

"You know," she said, "you could just ask him in class."

"Someone else might ask him first," Bat said.

"The chances of one of your classmates asking Israel to be partners for the class project between the parking lot and the classroom door are relatively low," Mom said.

"Low isn't zero," Bat answered.

Mom couldn't argue with this. They waited together, standing in front of the main entrance to the Saw Whet School, as the sea of arriving students and teachers parted around them. Bat counted six kids from his class—Jenny, Lucca, Ramon, Mei, Henry, and Starla. But none of them was Israel.

"Let's play a waiting game," Mom suggested. Waiting was one of the things that was very, very hard for Bat. Sometimes playing a game made time pass more quickly. But Bat was too excited about his good idea to play a game. He wanted to focus all his energy on waiting for Israel to arrive. He rubbed his thumb across the rough lump of clay skunk in his pocket.

Mr. Grayson pulled up in his dusty orange coupe and unfolded himself from its front seat. "Hey, Bat!" he said. "Are you waiting for me?"

"No," said Bat.

Mr. Grayson smiled, as if Bat had said something funny.

"Hi, Dr. Tam," he said to Bat's mom.

"Good morning, Mr. Grayson," she answered, and she put her hand on Bat's shoulder and gave it a little squeeze.

"Good morning, Mr. Grayson," Bat said, remembering to be polite, but he was craning his neck to see around his teacher, who was blocking his view of the parking lot entrance. Mr. Grayson's puffy orange vest looked like a traffic sign.

"Well," said Mr. Grayson, "I'll see you inside." He smiled again, and then finally he went into the building.

At last, Israel's dad's truck pulled into the parking lot. Israel's dad had the tallest, cleanest, shiniest truck Bat had ever seen in real life. Even the hubcaps shined.

Israel's dad waved at Bat and his mom as Israel hopped out of the passenger seat.

"Hey, Bat!" said Israel. He slammed the door and his dad drove away, the loud rumble of his truck fading.

"Do you want to be my partner for the spring project and research growing a skunk garden for Thor?" Bat didn't mean to yell right in Israel's face, but he had waited for so long that the words practically burst out of him.

"Sure! That sounds fun!" Israel grinned.

"Okay," said Bat. Then he turned to Mom. "Tell Laurence that Thor drank a bottle and a half for breakfast," he said. Laurence helped take care of the skunk kit during the day, when Bat was at school.

"I will," Mom said, and she bent down to give Bat a hug. "You boys have a great day."

Bat followed Israel through the school's front

door. The hallway was almost empty because class was about to start. There were just a few kids and Miss Kiko outside the kindergarten classroom, holding the copper bell she rang each morning to announce the start of school.

"Thanks for waiting for me," Israel said. "We were running late because Dad couldn't find the keys to his truck. He usually leaves them in a little dish by the front door, but—"

"We'll have to research what kinds of plants skunks like to eat," Bat interrupted. "Skunks are omnivores, which means they eat plants *and* animals, but I don't really know what kinds of plants taste the best to a skunk."

"Bat," Israel said, "I was telling you about why we were late!"

"You weren't late," Bat said. "You were *almost* late." And then he went into Mr. Grayson's class, before Miss Kiko rang the bell and they really *would* be late.

CHAPTER 6
Carrot Division

There wasn't any time to visit Babycakes before class began. Usually the first thing Bat did when he entered Mr. Grayson's classroom was head straight to the back to check on the class pet. Babycakes, a fluffy angora puffball of a bunny, usually didn't respond to Bat's gentle cooing; she'd just sit atop her plastic hutch inside her pen and look stoically adorable.

But today Bat had brought a carrot from home to feed to Babycakes, and she would always hop over for a carrot. If he hadn't been waiting outside of school for Israel to arrive, Bat would have had plenty of time to give the carrot to Babycakes. As it was, he would have to wait for recess.

Bat sighed as he slid into his chair, hanging his backpack over the back of the seat. The carrot, zipped into his backpack, seemed almost to vibrate with its desire to be fed to Babycakes.

Mr. Grayson was standing at the front of the room, talking about something. Bat saw his mouth moving but was having a very hard time concentrating on the words. Something about math. All around Bat, kids reached into their backpacks to pull out their folders, so Bat did, too.

There was the carrot, wrapped in a cloth napkin that was printed with little carrots and radishes and turnips. Bat retrieved his folder, but he grabbed the napkin-wrapped carrot, too.

Mr. Grayson's back was to the class. He was writing math problems on the whiteboard with his favorite orange marker.

It would only take a minute to walk to the back of the class and feed the carrot to Babycakes. Maybe Mr. Grayson wouldn't even turn back around until Bat had gone to Babycakes's enclosure, fed her the carrot, and returned to his seat.

And after all, Bat reasoned, Mr. Grayson *had* said that the class had an "open-door Babycakes policy," meaning that any time a kid needed to cuddle, he or she could go visit Babycakes, no permission needed, no questions asked. Bat didn't actually need to cuddle, but he had an itchy feeling that Babycakes needed the carrot, and he knew that the itchy feeling wouldn't go away until he did something about it.

So he unwrapped the carrot and pushed back his chair as quietly as he could. He tiptoed to the back of the class, ignoring the stares from Jenny and Lucca, and reached into the pen to feed the carrot to Babycakes.

Her twitchy nose twitched at the carrot, and Babycakes jumped down from her perch atop the plastic hutch and hopped over to Bat.

Silently, Bat held the carrot as Babycakes nibbled at it. She took little bites and chewed them quickly, her white face vibrating with joy.

"Bat," said Mr. Grayson's voice from just behind Bat's left shoulder. Bat jumped, startled, and his quick movement scared Babycakes, who darted into her hutch, just her fluffy tail sticking out.

"You made me scare Babycakes!" Bat said.

"She'll recover," Mr. Grayson said. "Do you think you could save the rest of her carrot until break? We are starting math time."

"I need to make sure Babycakes isn't upset," Bat said. "You can't just startle someone and not apologize." It occurred to Bat that maybe Mr. Grayson owed *him* an apology, for the same reason, but Mr. Grayson didn't offer one.

"Okay, Bat," Mr. Grayson said, but he didn't leave; he stood there waiting for Bat to go back to his seat.

Bat sighed. "Sorry, Babycakes," he said in his gentlest voice. Then he broke the carrot into three smaller pieces and set the pieces softly down inside the bunny's enclosure before he went back to his seat. Dividing one carrot into three parts: that, Bat thought, should count as math for the day.

CHAPTER 7
Good News and Bad News

After school, Bat and Mom were sitting at the kitchen table having a snack of sliced apples and cheddar cheese, waiting for Janie to get home. Bat liked to stack two slices of apple with one piece of cheese in between. It made for the perfect ratio of crunchiness and mushy saltiness. Thor was tucked into the sling around Bat's neck, but the little guy was rustling around more than usual, making the stacking procedure difficult.

"He's getting bigger," Mom said. "He's not quite a baby anymore. He's more like a toddler, and toddlers have lots of energy."

"What did you do with me when I was a toddler?" Bat asked.

"I made sure you got lots of exercise so you'd sleep at night," Mom answered.

Bat thought about this as he bit into his slightly crooked apple-cheese-apple sandwich. Thor needed more exercise. And as his caretaker, Bat's job was to make that happen.

"Maybe I'll build an obstacle course," Bat said, thinking out loud.

The front door slammed open, and Bat heard the stomping of two sets of feet coming down the hallway toward the kitchen. Janie and Ezra. He could tell it was them by the sound of their stomping—Janie's run was a sort of skip-hop sound, short quick steps close together. Ezra's was louder and more regular, and right behind Janie's.

"Guess what!" Janie yelled, bursting into the kitchen. Her cheeks were bright red from running, and her hair, which had been curly that morning, hung in limp ringlets around her face.

"You got the part of the queen in *Alice in Wonderland*," Bat said.

"Ba-at," Janie whined. "You ruined my news."

"You said to guess," said Bat.

"It was just an expression," said Ezra. He reached out and took an apple slice off Bat's plate, without even asking first. Bat pulled his plate a little closer. "Hi, Dr. Tam," Ezra said.

"Hello, Ezra," said Mom, and then to Janie, "Honey, that is wonderful news! Congratulations."

"Thanks," said Janie, shrugging out of her backpack and letting it drop to the floor by the back door. "I am so excited! Rehearsals start tomorrow after school."

"Tomorrow?" said Mom. "But tomorrow is Tuesday."

"We have rehearsal after school every day for the next three weeks," Janie said.

"Oh," Mom said. "Well, that throws a monkey wrench in our schedule."

Bat knew that Mom was using an expression, and that there wasn't really a wrench shaped like a monkey. But it felt satisfying when he imagined one, anyway.

"Usually you take care of Bat Tuesdays and Thursdays until I get home," Mom said.

"You're not going to tell me I can't do the play, are you?" Janie's voice was getting louder and higher, like the teakettle when it was just about to boil. "Because that would be totally unfair!"

"No, no, of course not," Mom said. "We'll work something out." Then she stood up and hugged Janie. "I'm so proud of you," she said. "Be sure to call your dad and tell him the good news. He'll be thrilled! Now, Ezra, would you like an apple of your own?"

Ezra, whose hand had been reaching out toward Bat's plate again, said, "Sure, Dr. Tam. And some cheese, too?"

· · ·

Later that day, after Ezra had gone home, after dinner and dishes and Thor's bedtime feeding, when Bat was brushing his teeth, Mom came into the bathroom and sat down on the edge of the bathtub.

"Bat," she said, "I want to ask you a question."

Bat hated it when people talked to him when he couldn't answer. Worst of all was at the dentist's, when he had his mouth wide open and the

dentist's rubber-gloved hands were in his mouth, and then she'd ask, "So, Bat, what grade are you in?" or "What's your favorite hobby these days, Bat?" and there was no way he could answer without biting her fingers.

Right now there weren't any fingers in his mouth, but there was a cheekful of foamy toothpaste. Bat spat it out and rinsed his mouth and then said, "What?"

"Your sister is going to be busy on Tuesdays and Thursdays for the next few weeks," Mom said, "and so we're going to have to change our schedule."

"I know," said Bat. "You're going to have to come home earlier."

"Well, no," Mom said. "I can't do that."

"Then I could come to the clinic," Bat said. "I could help Laurence."

"It's nice to have you at the clinic now and then,"

Mom said, "but maybe not quite that much. Also, you'll have your spring project to be working on."

And then she told Bat that she'd talked to Israel's dad, and that he had said that Bat could come over to their house for a few hours after school on Tuesdays and Thursdays, until Janie's play was over.

"You could ride home with them, they'd give you a snack, and you and Israel could work on your project. How does that sound?"

It sounded great—for exactly three seconds, until Bat remembered Thor.

"Can I bring Thor with me?" Bat asked.

"Oh, Bat," Mom answered. "I think that would be too much to ask of Israel's dad. Thor will have to stay with me at the clinic. Laurence will take care of him."

"That sounds like a terrible idea," Bat said. "Tell

Janie she can't do the play."

"Bat," Mom said. "That doesn't seem fair, does it? And it's just for a couple of hours, only on Tuesdays and Thursdays, and only for a few weeks. We can do this, Bat, can't we?"

Bat thrust his toothbrush back in the holder and wiped his mouth with the hand towel. He remembered something Mom sometimes said to him and turned to her. "Just because we *can* do something," he said, "doesn't mean we *should*."

CHAPTER 8
Kitchens

There were some terrible things about Bat's new after-school schedule:

1. The extra time away from Thor.
2. The uncomfortable feeling of going to a new place, itching Bat like the heat rash he sometimes got on summer's hottest days.
3. The inconvenience of being away from his very own home, his perfectly comfortable room.

But, Bat had to admit the next afternoon, staring up at Israel's dad's massive, rumbling black truck, the ride wasn't one of them.

Bat had never been in such an interesting vehicle. Mom drove a perfectly average station wagon, and Dad had an uncomfortably tight sports car, with a hump in the middle of the back instead of a seat.

Israel's dad's truck was totally different. It was like seeing a Great Dane after a lifetime of Chihuahuas. It was the ostrich of the car world: impressively large.

Tuesday's school day had ended, and when Bat and Israel walked out of the building to the pickup line, Bat immediately spotted the truck.

"I think that's the coolest truck I've ever seen," Bat said to Israel.

"I didn't know you cared about trucks," Israel said.

"Neither did I," said Bat.

"Hi, boys," said Israel's dad through the open window as he pulled up to the front of the line. He leaned over and unlocked the passenger-side door. "Hop in!"

The truck was so tall that Bat had to use the chrome bar that ran beneath the door to step up and climb in. Standing on the bar, peering into the cab of the truck, Bat found himself at a loss for words. It had never, ever occurred to Bat to care the least bit about a vehicle. He liked fur and feathers and scales, teeth and claws and tails.

The truck was just chrome and paint and rubber and steel, but somehow it felt *alive*, and peering into its cab was like looking into the heart of a dragon.

"I like your truck, Mr. Zimmerman," Bat said.

"Thank you, Bat," he answered. "Call me Tom."

"Tom," Bat said, half to himself, as Israel's dad

pulled forward the front passenger seat so the boys could climb onto the narrow rear bench. It had, Bat noticed with satisfaction, three seat belts. He plopped himself happily in the center seat, latched his belt, and said to Tom, "Tell me every-thing about this truck."

By the time they pulled into Israel's driveway ten minutes later, Bat knew the difference between a V-8 and a V-6 engine, he knew what a drivetrain was and why it was better to have four-wheel drive than two-wheel drive, he knew that Tom's truck could tow up to twelve thousand pounds ("give or take a few," Tom said), and he knew with 99 percent surety (because that was as sure as you could be about anything) that one day he would drive a truck exactly like Israel's dad's.

Tom put the car in park and turned it off. "Here we are," he said, which normally would have prompted Bat to say something about how that was the kind of statement that really didn't mean anything, because it's always true—you could always say "Here we are," no matter where you were, and you'd be right. But Bat didn't point that out, this time.

"Thank you for driving us," he said instead, remembering his manners, like Mom had told him to try to do.

"Anytime," Tom answered. And then he said, "You're a cool kid, Bat."

That was definitely the first time anyone had ever called Bat "cool."

Bat followed Israel into the house, putting his backpack on the kitchen counter next to where Israel set his.

Bat looked around as Israel slammed open the pantry and rustled through it, looking for a snack. It was a very different kitchen than the two kitchens Bat was most used to. His kitchen at home had mostly empty countertops tiled in plain white squares. There was a bowl of fruit and a toaster, and that was about it. Everything else Mom kept put away; as she said, "habit from keeping a clean operating room." The kitchen at Dad's apartment was pretty empty, too, but for a different reason: he had only lived in the apartment for a year and a half, and he didn't really have much stuff.

Israel's kitchen would have made a terrible operating room. The countertops were blue, but it was hard to tell under all the stacks of colorful ceramic bowls and cups and plates that were piled all over them. The walls were light yellow, but it was hard to tell under the pictures that were hanging—some framed, some loose taped-up sketches—all over them.

Israel emerged from the pantry with a bag of pistachio nuts, a box of cereal, and a chocolate bar. "Do you want a snack?" he said to Bat, the first words he'd spoken since they'd left school. "Or do you just want to go hang out with my dad some more?"

The chocolate bar looked delicious. "Snack, please," Bat said.

CHAPTER 9
Bowls

Bat had never eaten a bowl of cereal without milk before, but Israel poured half the box into a big gray-and-pink bowl and then poured a bunch of pistachios into a slightly smaller green bowl with swirly blue curlicues all over it. Then he put away the cereal box and the bag of pistachios, told Bat, "Grab the chocolate bar," and headed out into the backyard.

Bat, chocolate bar in hand, followed him.

"Wow," he said, standing in the doorway, look-ing into the yard. Israel was placing the two fancy bowls full of snacks on a table underneath a big shade tree, but that was the least interesting thing happening in the yard.

Bat counted eleven pinwheel wind spinners planted in the garden beds all around the yard. Some had bits of colored glass suspended in webs of metal; others were all metal, but a mix of cop-per and silver. Big, bright glass orbs were tucked everywhere, glints of shiny color under the tree, lining the path through the yard that ended at a garden shed.

The shade tree's branches were heavy with stained-glass ornaments and wind chimes that filled the air with silvery tinkles and deep, vibrat-ing clangs. There was so much to see and hear that Bat felt caught between it all. The colors, the sounds, the newness of everything.

Suddenly, despite the beauty and excitement of Israel's amazing backyard, Bat wished desperately that he were home.

"Hey," Israel said. "Are you okay?"

Bat felt himself bouncing on the balls of his feet, and he knew his eyes were full of tears. He still clutched the chocolate bar in his hand.

"Sort of not really," he said.

Israel scratched his head. "Come on," he said, taking the chocolate bar from Bat and setting it on the table. "I'll introduce you to my mom."

But instead of leading Bat into the house, Israel walked through the garden to the shed. As they crossed the yard, Bat took deep calming breaths and wiped his eyes. The shed door was open, and as he got closer Bat saw that it wasn't just a place to store shovels and rakes.

"Hey, Mom," said Israel.

"You're home!" came a voice from inside the shed. "Is your friend with you?"

"Yep," said Israel. "Bat, come say hi to my mom."

Bat peered into the shed. Israel's mom was in there, surrounded by shelves full of bowls and cups and plates and pots, some glazed in bright colors, others the flat gray of unfinished clay.

She was sitting behind a potter's wheel, a lump of wet clay in her hands. Splatters of clay decorated her arms and her overalls.

"Hi, Bat," she said. "I'm Cora."

"Hello," said Bat. "What are you doing?"

"I'm making a bowl," Cora said. "Do you want to try?"

Bat shook his head. "I don't like slimy things," he said. "Or sticky things." He looked around at all the shelves and all the things upon them. "Did you make all this stuff?"

"Most of it," Cora said. "Over there is Israel's work."

The shelf she pointed to was filled with lumps of clay that looked a lot like the lump of clay Israel had made for Bat, which Bat had right then tucked into the pocket of his vest.

"Mom's stuff is better than mine," Israel said. "She's a professional artist. I'm just starting out."

Bat looked back and forth between the pottery Cora had made and the awkward lumps Israel had made. "Yes," he said. "Your mom's stuff is way better."

Israel crossed his arms across his chest.

Bat felt his stomach rumble and said, "I think I'm ready for that snack now."

CHAPTER 10
Missing Connections

Mom's perfectly average station wagon felt decidedly less than average that evening when she collected Bat from Israel's house.

"So, how was it?" Mom asked, putting the car in reverse to back down the driveway.

"Mom," Bat said, "have you ever thought about getting a truck?"

"A truck?" Mom said. She shifted into drive and stepped on the gas.

"Yes," said Bat. "A big one."

"Actually," Mom said, "the first car I bought, when I was eighteen years old, was a truck."

"Really? Was it like Tom's truck?"

"Tom?" asked Mom, glancing over at Bat.

"Israel's dad," said Bat.

"Ah. I didn't realize you were on a first-name basis."

"It's no big deal," Bat said. "Tom is cool."

Mom laughed. "Careful, or you might make me jealous! You've never called *me* cool. Anyway," she said, "did you have a good time with Israel?"

"Mm-hmm," said Bat. Then he realized that he hadn't yet asked about Thor. "Oh!" he said. "Is Thor okay? Did you remember to give him his four-o'clock feeding?"

"Of course I did," Mom said. She flicked on her turn signal and made a right onto their street, Plum Lane. "Thor is great. He's in the back."

"You put Thor in the *trunk*?" Bat's voice went high and squeaky with indignation.

"He's just fine," Mom said, and she pulled into their driveway, put the car in park, and turned the key.

Bat unlatched his seat belt, threw open his car door, and ran around to the back of the car. He clicked open the rear door and pushed it up. "Ooh," he said.

There was Thor's travel carrier, a secondhand cat kennel, but there was something else back there, too—a plastic gate, or fence, or something.

"It's a doggy pen," Mom said. "Someone donated it to the clinic today, and I thought we could use it for Thor. What do you think? Want to help me set it up?"

This pen, Bat thought, was even cooler than Tom's truck.

· · ·

They got the sections of the pen—four plastic sides,
it turned out, to form a square—into the house.
Mom tried to set the two pieces she was carrying
down in the living room, but Bat carried his two
sections all the way down the hallway and into
his bedroom, where he intended to build it. Then
he immediately started trying to figure out how
to connect them together.

"We can do it later, Bat," Mom said, standing in
the doorway of his room. "After dinner and bath
time."

"I want to do it now," Bat said, all his concen-
tration on hooking the pieces together. He could
see, though, that something was missing. The two
plastic panels just wouldn't latch together. "Are
there any more parts?" he asked.

"I don't think so," Mom said, and she came

into Bat's room to see what the problem was. "Oh. There must be connecting rods that slip into the edges here to hold the sections together. I don't know, Bat. Maybe they're at the clinic and I just didn't see them."

"We have to go back to the clinic and find them," Bat said.

"Not tonight, honey. It's getting late. We're all done being out in the world for the day."

"We have to build the pen for Thor!" Bat felt the anxious knot tightening in his chest the way it sometimes did. He knew he should walk away from the problem and take deep calming breaths, but he didn't *want* to walk away from the problem and take deep calming breaths. He wanted to *fix* the problem.

"Bat," said Mom, "you've had a long day, haven't you?" She knelt down beside him and took his hands in hers. She squeezed his hands and released, her signal to him that she was going to try to help him calm down. If he didn't want the help, Bat knew he could take a step away, but he stayed still. His mom moved her hands to his wrists and squeezed and released, and then she worked her way up his arms, squeezing his forearms and his elbows and his biceps and his shoulders, and then working her way back down to his hands. "Baby," she said, and it was this word that pushed Bat over the edge.

He *wasn't* a baby. He wasn't anywhere *close* to being a baby. Thor was a baby, and Bat was his caretaker, and right now he wanted to take care of Thor by building this playpen, and if that meant going back to the clinic even though it was closed for the day, then that is what they should do, and Bat didn't understand why Mom couldn't see how important this was and how right he was and just DO WHAT HE WANTED HER TO DO.

"Bat, honey, shhh," Mom said, and that's when Bat heard the sound he was making. He hadn't even noticed that he'd started making the sound, the high-pitched whine that seemed to come out of him when he was the most upset, when he had "reached the end of his rope," as Mom called it.

But even though he hated making the noise, it felt good to make it, too, just as it felt good to bounce on the soles of his feet. Mom's hands were still squeezing Bat's arms, and then she put her arms around him, pulling him close, and she held him just like that, in a nice tight hug, and Bat wanted at the same time to pull away from her and to never be let go.

She held him until he stopped needing to make high-pitched whining sounds, until he stopped needing to bounce on the soles of his feet, until the knot in his chest began to relax and unwind.

Then she said very softly, "Come on, Bat. Let me run a bath for you."

And Bat let her lead him away from the pen.

CHAPTER 11
Bananafish

//

After bath time, Bat pulled on his pajamas and went into the kitchen, where he found Mom and Janie together at the table, having breakfast for dinner, which they sometimes did when there hadn't been time to fix a bigger meal.

Janie was having fried eggs, and Mom was spooning out two platefuls of scrambled—one for Bat and one for herself. Bat did not like runny eggs. He didn't even like it when other people ate runny eggs, because then he had to witness it. But Janie liked to dip buttered toast into the little pool of yellow yolk, and she was Bat's sister, so sometimes witnessing such a thing was unavoidable.

The bath had helped Bat to feel calmer. Still warm from sitting in the steaming water, he drifted to his seat at the table and decided that Janie's disgusting eggs were something he could overlook tonight.

"We have a week and a half to memorize our lines," Janie said to Mom, diving the edge of her triangle-cut toast into the yolk stream. "By the Tuesday after next, the director wants the whole rehearsal to run without any scripts."

Bat piled a forkful of scrambled egg onto his toast. "How do you guys know where to stand and stuff?" he asked.

"That's called blocking," Janie said enthusiastically. "We have to write it all down in our scripts—when to come on stage, and which side we come in from, and where we go, and when we sit down or stand up or whatever."

"That sounds like a lot to remember," Bat said.

"Oh, it is," Janie said. "But that's all right. I'm good at it. You probably would be good at that part too, Bat. You're good at remembering things."

Bat finished his scrambled eggs and imagined himself on stage, surrounded by other kids, acting out the words from a script. He didn't really know how it all worked, so the things he imagined were fuzzy and vague. But they still made him feel nervous. "I could probably memorize the stuff," he said, "but I wouldn't want to be on stage. With all those people watching."

"I love it," Janie said. "I was born for the spotlight."

A bright light shining right on him, while rows of people sat and stared. That sounded like some kind of punishment to Bat.

"There's room in a theater for the performers *and* the audience," Mom said. "A show isn't a show without both. Bat and I will be your audience. Won't we, Bat?"

Bat nodded. "Yes," he said.

"But tonight," Mom said, clearing away the plates and stacking them in the sink, "what do the two of you say to a game of Bananafish?"

They both said yes to Bananafish, which was a game Janie had made up when Bat was little. Well, Bat had thought that she had made it up. When he was older, he found out that the game she called Bananafish was the game most everyone else called War. The only difference was that instead of saying "War!" when two people flipped over matching cards, you were supposed to call out "Bananafish!"

You could play with two or three or even four

players, which was perfect for their family. Janie shuffled the cards and dealt them into three equal stacks while Bat loaded the dishwasher and Mom heated up some milk and cocoa in the red saucepan, pouring it into three mugs when it was just the right temperature. They settled into companionable silence and began flipping over cards, whoever had the highest card taking all three.

After four rounds, the first match turned up—Janie and Bat each flipped over a seven. "Bananafish!" they yelled, and then dealt three cards face down, waited a moment, and then flipped a fourth card face up.

Janie's was a six. Bat's was a queen.

"Bananafish!" he called again, this time in triumph.

"Good one, Bat," Janie said nicely, and he smiled.

"Thanks," he said. And then, even though he

knew the answer, he asked, "Janie, why did you call this game Bananafish?" He liked to hear the story every time they played.

"Because when you were little, it was hard to get you to play new games with me. You only liked to do the things you already knew how to do. And I begged and begged for you to let me teach you how to play War, but you always said no. And then one day I asked you if you wanted to learn how to play a new game called Bananafish, because 'banana' and 'fish' were two of your favorite words."

"Even though I didn't like banana-flavored yogurt," Bat added happily.

"And you said yes to playing Bananafish, even though it was the exact same game you'd been saying no to playing, only with a different name."

"It's important to know your audience," Mom said. All three of them flipped over another card. Mom's jack was higher than Janie's nine and Bat's four, so she took all three.

Bat didn't remember the day that Janie taught him Bananafish. But he thought Janie had been pretty smart for getting him to play her game after all. "Since I wanted to play after you named the game Bananafish," he said, "maybe I didn't want to play because it was called War. That's a word I don't like."

"I agree," Mom said.

"That makes three," Janie said. "Bananafish are definitely better than War."

Bananafish are better than War. And being together, cozy in their kitchen, was better than being apart.

CHAPTER 12
A Perfect Night

Friday after school, Bat climbed into Dad's little sports car, sliding over to behind the driver's seat since there was no seat belt in the middle. Dad was whistling, something Bat liked and something that sort of amazed him. No matter how he tried, Bat couldn't arrange his lips into a proper whistling position.

"How was your week, sport?" Dad asked as he pulled out of the school parking lot.

"It was okay," said Bat. "Not great." Thursday's after-school visit to Israel's house, when Bat had hoped they would research possible vegetables for their skunk garden project, had instead been spent sitting on the couch while Israel played his new video game and practically ignored him.

And though they had finally gotten the pen built, and though Mom had agreed to let Bat keep it in his room, Bat felt terribly irritated about the fact that this was an Every-Other Weekend. Even worse, this would be his first Every-Other Weekend without Janie, because she had rehearsal today and tomorrow and a sleepover with a castmate on Saturday night.

"I've got a surprise for you," Dad said.

"Is it that you've decided to let Thor spend the weekend with me at your apartment?" Bat said, hopeful.

"No," said Dad. "It's baseball tickets!"

Bat slumped in his seat, defeated. Baseball tickets. It was like his dad was trying to punish him for something.

There was almost nothing good about a baseball game, but Bat could nearly make a game out of listing all the things that were bad about one:

1. The lines. Lines to park the car, lines to get through the entry gate, lines to use the bathroom, lines to buy snacks and drinks, lines to get to your seats. Bat hated waiting in lines. He hated it *so much*.

2. The crowds. Even when you weren't waiting in a line, you were still surrounded by people. Too many bodies squished together into too small a space. The smell of the bodies. People said *skunks* smell bad! That wasn't even true. Skunks only smelled bad when they sprayed.

Some of the people at a baseball game seemed to smell all the time.

3. The lights. All those bright-white fluorescent bulbs, flooding the field in their artificial glare, making Bat's eyes feel twitchy.

4. The noise. Oh, the noise. People shouting at the peanut guy. People laughing loudly to each other and calling out to their friends. The announcer over the loudspeaker, booming out information that seemed to Bat to be totally unnecessary. The music. The crowds bursting into cheers when a batter scored a run.

Bat loved his dad. He really did. But when his dad made him do something like this, like coming to a baseball game, something he really didn't want to do, Bat wondered if his dad understood him.

Because if his dad really understood him, then

he would understand that an event like a baseball game was just about the worst way that Bat could imagine spending a Saturday night.

"We've got good seats, sport!" Dad said, dragging Bat down the aisle and pushing enthusiastically through the crowd. "Excuse us! Pardon us!" he said.

The seats didn't look good to Bat. They were too close to the field, which meant that there was a higher chance that a stray baseball could hit him in the face.

"What do you think?" Dad asked after they were settled onto the uncomfortable blue plastic fold-down chairs.

"Can we go home?" Bat asked.

"Don't be silly," Dad said. "They're just taking batting practice. The game hasn't even started yet!"

Bat didn't want the game to start. He wanted the game to be canceled. But, in all the years Dad had been making Bat go to baseball games, only one of them had been canceled, and that was on account of rain.

Bat looked up into the cloudless, clear sky. The horizon was melting into pink and orange as the sun slipped away for the night. It was a beautiful, perfect evening. Bat sighed and shook his head. It was going to be a long night.

CHAPTER 13
Seventh-Inning Stretch

By the seventh-inning stretch, Bat's whole body felt twitchy from sitting. Dad *loved* the seventh-inning stretch. He called it "a fun tradition."

Bat thought of the seventh-inning stretch as the earliest possible opportunity to get Dad to leave a baseball game. If the score wasn't close, sometimes Bat could convince Dad to head home after everyone finished singing "Take Me Out to the Ball Game."

The seventh-inning stretch happened after one team had had its turn at bat but before the other team came out to hit. All the players left the field, and everyone in the stands got on their feet. The big screens lit up with the lyrics to the song, and the organ music began, playing loudly through the PA system. Then a little animated baseball bounced along over the words just in case anyone didn't know how the song went.

Dad dropped his arm across Bat's shoulders and began to sway back and forth to the tune, swaying Bat along with him.

"Take me out to the ball game," sang the crowd all around Bat. Down on the field, the mascot—a man in a giant bird costume—jumped around, waving his wings to encourage the crowd to sing louder.

"If they don't win it's a shame," boomed Dad. Bat folded his arms across his chest and wished he had his earmuffs.

At last the song was over and everyone settled back into their seats. The score, Bat saw on the big, lighted scoreboard, was 3–2. The home team was winning. There was no way Dad would want to leave yet. Still, it was worth a try.

"If we go now, we could beat the traffic out of the parking lot," Bat said.

"And miss the end? No way!" Dad said. "Hey, do you want another hot dog?"

Bat shook his head. He had already eaten two hot dogs and a bunch of popcorn and was feeling slightly sick. He slumped down in his seat, resigned to staying for the rest of the game.

Dad straightened the baseball cap on Bat's head, which was an exact match to the cap Dad was wearing, and which Dad had just given him that day. "You know, sport, you could try a little harder to enjoy the things I'm interested in. It's a good talent, learning to appreciate other people's interests."

"Well," said Bat, "you don't try very hard to appreciate *my* interests! You haven't even met Thor, and he's the most interesting thing in my life."

Dad didn't say anything for a while. The teams jogged back onto the field and took their positions. The fielding team threw the ball around to warm up, and then the batter came to home plate and the game started up again.

Just when Bat thought that maybe Dad hadn't heard him at all, he said, "You know, sport, you're right. I should have met that little fellow by now. I'm sorry it's taken me so long. But I'll tell you what. You let me tell you a few things about baseball and try your best to enjoy the rest of this game, and then tomorrow when I drop you off with your mom, we'll spend some time together with Thor. How does that sound?"

Bat smiled. It sounded good.

"Okay," Dad said as they settled back into their seats after a final visit to the concession stand (though Bat had no more room for hot dogs, he found he could make a little space for cotton

candy). "Let me tell you a few things that I love about baseball games. Starting with the most important part."

"The stats?" Bat guessed. He knew how much Dad loved keeping track of the players' statistics: batting, pitching, fielding, base running. Dad had a whole stack of notebooks that he kept in the top drawer of his desk, dedicated to keeping track of statistics.

"The stats are pretty great," Dad said. "But it's not the stats that I like best."

"Is it the hats?" Bat asked. Dad had a shelf in his closet where he kept his collection of baseball caps. He liked to wear the cap of whatever team he was cheering for, whether he was at the game or watching it on TV.

"It's not the hats," Dad said.

"The food?"

"Nope."

"The crowds?"

"No."

"The mascots?"

Dad laughed. "It's not the mascots."

"I give up," Bat said. "What's your favorite thing about baseball?"

"It's this," Dad said, relaxing in his seat and putting his arm around Bat's shoulders again. "This, right here. Sitting next to someone I love, having a snack and something to drink, enjoying the outside air together. Spending time together. Being with you."

Bat could point out to Dad that they could do most of these things back at the apartment, or at the park. It didn't have to be at a baseball game. Technically, Dad's argument was flawed. But instead of pointing this out, Bat paid attention to the pleasant warmth and weight of Dad's arm across his shoulders. He pinched off some cotton candy and popped it into his mouth, enjoying the way it changed from fluff into melting sweetness. He looked out across the field, not trying to keep track of the players or the score. Instead he tried to melt a little, like the cotton candy, and just be happy to be right there at the game with his dad.

The moment was sweet. Not quite as sweet as cotton candy, but pretty close.

CHAPTER 14
Yarrow and Sloke

At school on Monday, Bat and Israel got to use Mr. Grayson's computer to research the best vegetables for a skunk diet. They found a website that had sample menus for skunks. It said that young skunks, once weaned from formula, should be fed four times per day and should get a mixture of vegetables, a protein like chicken or fish, some sort of grain or crushed-up nuts, and occasionally some fruit for a treat.

"It sounds like a regular person diet," Israel said.

"Well, skunks *are* omnivores, like people." Bat wished the website had a list of the vegetables that taste the best to skunks, but all it said was "mixed vegetables, frozen or fresh."

"So what do you want to plant?" Israel asked.

"I don't know," Bat said. "What are your favorite vegetables?"

"I like avocados," Israel said.

"Avocados are fruit, and they're from trees," Bat said. "We can't grow those in a garden box."

"Oh," said Israel. And then he said, "Hey! I have a great idea!"

Israel's idea was to make a survey for the class to take, asking everyone to write down their five favorite vegetables. "Then we can figure out which vegetables are the most popular, and we can plant those," he said.

Bat nodded. "I like it," he said. "Very scientific."

When they told Mr. Grayson Israel's idea, he said, "You can use the copy machine in the office if you want!"

So Bat and Israel made a survey:

Pick your three favorite vegetables from this list. Number them 1, 2, and 3.

Asparagus

Brussels Sprouts

Broccoli

Cabbage

Carrot

Corn

Kale

Lettuce

Spinach

Squash

Bat wanted to include every vegetable they found on a website that listed all the vegetables in alphabetical order, but Israel said, "I don't think anyone in our class knows what yarrow or sloke even *are*, Bat!"

So Bat compromised on just ten. Then they took the hall pass, which was an old flip-flop with "Walking Pass" written on the sole, and headed to the front office to make their copies.

"Well, hello, boys," said Principal Martinez. "What can we do for you?"

"Hi, Principal," said Israel. "Mr. Grayson said we could use the copy machine. Look! We're doing a survey." He gave her the sheet they'd written up.

"I see," said Principal Martinez. "Very interesting. Do you need me to show you how to work the machine?"

"No," said Bat. "I know how. My mom has a copy machine at her clinic that she sometimes lets me use."

"Okay," said the principal. "Well, good luck with your survey!"

"Thank you," said Israel, but Bat was already on his way to the machine.

"Bat, you should have said thank you," Israel whispered to him loudly as Bat entered sixteen—the number of students in their class—into the copy machine's display.

"Do you think sixteen copies is enough?" Bat asked.

"Make it eighteen, just in case."

Bat made it eighteen. He and Israel stood next to each other and watched the identical copies of their survey emerge one by one from the machine. It was, Bat thought, very satisfying. Also, Bat loved the way a working copy machine smelled—hot, kind of rubbery, important.

When the machine was done, Bat took the copies plus the original, tapped the papers into a neat stack, and said, "There."

"I wonder what the winners will be," Israel said as they walked back to class.

"I hope kale is in the top three," Bat said.

"Why?" asked Israel. "Do you like kale?"

"Not really," Bat said. "But my mom says it's got lots of vitamins in it, and I want Thor to be extra healthy."

When they got back to class, Mr. Grayson said, "Okay, everyone! Attention! We have a special activity. Bat, Israel, want to tell us about it?"

Bat opened his mouth to talk, but nothing came out. It was as if, standing in front of the class with everyone staring at him, he had forgotten how to speak.

Luckily, Israel remembered. "Bat and I are going to plant a garden to grow food for Thor, the skunk Bat's raising. And we want everyone to vote on which vegetables we should plant. So everyone take a survey and mark your three favorite vegetables."

Then he nudged Bat, who was holding the stack of surveys. Jolted into movement, Bat passed them out. He even gave one to Mr. Grayson and one to Israel, and kept one for himself.

Back at his desk, on his own survey, Bat

numbered kale, broccoli, and corn as one, two, and three. When everyone was done, he and Israel walked around the room and collected the surveys.

"Okay!" said Mr. Grayson. "When you've tallied the results, let us know what the winning vegetables are!" Then it was time for recess, and everyone went outside. Bat stared down at the stack of surveys, smiling. They were really going to make a skunk garden.

CHAPTER 15
Thor's Garden

"Carrots, corn, and kale!" Bat told Mom on the drive home from school.

"Carrots, corn, and kale!" Bat told Janie when she got home, interrupting the song she was singing.

"Carrots, corn, and kale," Bat whispered to Thor as he fed him his afternoon bottle, cradling his squirming, eager black-and-white body. Thor was getting *strong,* Bat noticed. He filled Bat's hands now, and his snuffling snout pushed into Bat's palm as he searched for the bottle.

"I think your little friend is ready for solid food," Mom said. She was in the kitchen with Bat, drinking a cup of tea and watching him feed the kit.

"Carrots, corn, and kale!" Bat said again.

"Yes," said Mom. "Those sound like great choices for a skunk garden. But in the meantime, let's try something a little easier to digest." She set down her tea and took a slice of bread from the loaf by the toaster. She pulled away the crusts and cut just the softest center of the slice into little cubes. Then she dripped some of the formula onto the plate of bread cubes and waited until it had soaked in and the bread was soft. Then she set the plate on the floor and said, "Let's see what he thinks."

Bat sat on the floor and made a V with his legs

around the plate of bread. Gently, he set Thor down. At first, the little kit stumbled as he got his legs underneath him, but his tiny nose went up like he smelled the food and he wove his way over to the plate, his tail bushy behind him.

When he got to the plate of bread, he sniffed around for a while. Bat didn't know if he would eat it. "Maybe he doesn't like bread," he said to Mom.

"Give him a minute," Mom said. She had sat down on the floor, too, right next to Bat, and they watched together as Thor climbed up onto the plate with his front legs and dipped his mouth down toward the food.

Sniff, sniff, sniff. Then, his tongue emerged and touched the bread. Then he licked it. Then he got even closer, opened his mouth, and took a bite.

"He's eating!" Bat said.

"He sure is," Mom said.

Thor chomped down half the plate of formula-soaked bread, and then he turned away from it. Bat scooped him up and wiped his face clean with a napkin Mom handed him.

"They grow up so fast, don't they, Bat?" Mom said.

Bat nodded. He was proud of Thor, but he knew what it meant that Thor was learning to eat on his own. It meant that he was one step closer to being able to return to the wild—one step closer to not needing Bat anymore.

"I kind of wish he still needed to be bottle-fed," Bat said.

"Babies can't stay babies forever," Mom said. She stroked Bat's hair as he stroked Thor.

• • •

Thursday afternoon, Bat and Tom and Israel took the big black truck to the nursery to get supplies for the skunk garden. Bat and Israel had written up a list of supplies, and Mom had checked it the night before. She'd crossed off "shovel" and "hoe" because she said they already had those things in the shed.

That still left: carrot seeds, corn seeds, kale seeds, and fertilizer. Not a very exciting list. When they'd found everything they needed, Tom drove them all back to Bat's house so that they could get to work.

Bat had never been at his house without another member of his family being there, and he wished suddenly that Janie were home. Not because he wanted her to make him a sandwich, not because he needed anything from her—just because it would have been nice to have her there.

He found the key just where Mom had promised to leave it, under the second-biggest potted plant on the front porch (because the biggest one was too heavy to move), and used it to open the front door. Then, standing in the hallway with Tom and Israel, Bat felt suddenly shy.

But Israel raced straight through to the kitchen, down the steps, and into the backyard. "Come on, Bat! Let's garden!"

Half an hour later, the garden box was planted. Tom had found a couple of pieces of wood and some old paint in the shed, and when Bat and Israel were done smoothing over the dirt, he said, "What do you boys think of this?"

It was a signpost that read "Thor's Garden."

"It's perfect," said Bat.

Tom hammered the sign into the dirt and they all stood together admiring it. Now they just had to wait for the plants to grow.

CHAPTER 16
Sleepover

"Do you think there's time to bake cookies before they get here?" Janie asked Mom. She had been working all day on getting ready for her big sleepover party. Three friends from her school musical were going to arrive any minute, and Bat had been watching her flurry of preparation with curiosity and maybe just a touch of jealousy.

"You already made brownies and ordered pizzas

and had Mom take you to the store for three different kinds of juice," Bat said, thinking that with three different kinds of juice, Janie shouldn't be so selfish about not letting him open even *one* until the guests arrived.

"I know," Janie said, twirling her hair up into a bun. "But I can't remember if Corinna said she doesn't like brownies or cookies. I *thought* it was cookies she doesn't like, so I made brownies, but now I think I might be remembering wrong."

"I like brownies," Bat said, "and I also like cookies."

"I know, Bat," Janie said, rolling her eyes.

Bat hated when Janie rolled her eyes at him. It was rude. He was about to tell her so when the doorbell rang.

"They're here!" Janie yelped, and she ran out of the kitchen.

Soon the house was brimming with noise. Janie and her friends seemed to have forgotten the whole concept of "inside voices." Bat peeked through the kitchen door. One of Janie's friends saw him and waved. Bat waved back, then headed down the hall toward his room.

"Janie," he heard a girl's voice ask, "didn't you tell me your brother is autistic?"

"Uh-huh," said Janie.

"So is my cousin," the girl answered.

Bat went into his room and closed the door firmly behind him, but he could still hear the girls, only slightly muffled.

Bat sighed and flopped down into his beanbag. He wasn't sure what name to give the emotion he was feeling. His eyes darted around his room as he looked for something to do. Even his animal encyclopedia, which usually made him perfectly content, didn't seem appealing. And Thor must have been deep into his afternoon nap, because Bat couldn't hear him stirring in his enclosure.

Now that Thor was less of a baby and more of a toddler, Bat liked to think of his enclosure as a playpen. In one back corner was the kitty transport box that made a sort of cave for Thor to sleep in; in the other back corner, newspapers acted as a bathroom for the kit, who was quickly learning the right place to go; up toward the gate at the front was Thor's food dish, which Bat filled four times a day, and a water dish, which he changed and refilled every morning and night. Hanging from the gate was Thor's sling, which he used to disappear into but which was getting a little tight.

Mom knocked on Bat's door. He knew it was her because she always knocked in a little pattern—knock-knock, pause, knock.

"Come in," he said.

Mom opened the door, and the girls' noise got

louder. She came into the room and shut the door again. "Those girls know how to party," she said with a smile.

Bat shrugged. "I guess," he said.

Mom sat on the edge of the bed. "How's Thor?"

"He's taking his nap," Bat sighed, and for no reason his eyes filled with tears.

"Oh, little Bat," said Mom, and she stroked his hair. "Are you feeling lonely?"

Bat shrugged. "Maybe," he said.

Mom pet Bat's hair in long, slow strokes. It felt nice. "Hey," she said. "I have an idea."

"What?" said Bat.

"Do you want to call Israel and see if he'd like to come for a sleepover? We could break out your trundle bed," Mom said.

Bat had had a trundle bed as long as he could remember, but the only person who had ever slept on it was Janie when they were younger and he could sometimes talk her into sleeping in his room.

"Do you think he'd want to?" Bat asked.

"Only one way to find out," Mom said.

It turned out that Israel *did* want to come for a sleepover. Sometimes life meant lots of waiting and not knowing, but this time everything happened fast: Israel answered the phone on the second ring, and he said "Yes!" as soon as Bat asked him if he wanted to come over, and then Bat's mom talked to Israel's mom, and within half an hour, it was Bat's turn to open the door when the doorbell rang, and it was *his* friend standing on the front porch holding a pillow and a knapsack.

"Hi," said Bat. "Do you like brownies?"

"They're my favorite," Israel said with a grin, and then he came inside.

CHAPTER 17
Party Games

//

"Hey, do you want to play a game with us?" Janie had opened the door without knocking, which she knew wasn't allowed.

"You forgot to knock," Bat said.

Janie rolled her eyes. "Okay, then I guess you don't want to play with us," she said, and began to close the door.

"Wait, wait!" Israel said, jumping to his feet. "I want to play!" He followed Janie into the hallway, turning to say, "Come on, Bat!"

Bat checked on Thor before he followed. Inside the playpen, inside the kitty carrier, the tip of the skunk's tail poked out from the flannel blanket that Thor liked to sleep inside. Bat closed the bedroom door behind him and followed Israel and Janie down the hall.

The living room was a mess. Janie's three friends sat on a nest they'd made of all the couch cushions; the coffee table was shoved to one side, paper plates of half-eaten pizza and paper cups full of juice littered all over it.

"So this is my brother, Bat, and his friend Israel," Janie said. "And these are my friends Corinna, Maggie, and Frida." She pointed at each of the three girls as she said their names.

"Um, hi," said Israel, with a little wave. Then he elbowed Bat.

"Ouch," Bat said.

"Say hello," Israel whispered loudly.

"Hello," Bat said.

"Oh, your brother is *adorable*, Janie," said one of the girls—Maggie—from the pillow pile.

Bat's face felt hot and prickly, and he shifted his weight from foot to foot.

"Are you guys going to play with us?" said Frida.

"What's the game?" said Israel. His voice sounded unusually squeaky to Bat.

"It's called Two Truths and a Lie. Have you ever played?" Janie asked.

Bat shook his head no. So did Israel.

"It's fun," said Frida. "You just think of two things that are true about you and one lie. Then you say all three of them and try to hide which one is a lie. Then everyone guesses which one the lie is, and if you fool everyone, you get a prize."

"What's the prize?" asked Bat.

"A bag of gummies," Janie said, holding up a clear plastic bag full of gummies.

"Okay," said Israel. "We'll play." He flopped down on one of the cushions. Bat sat next to him.

"I'll go first," said Maggie. Like the other girls, she was dressed in pajamas. Maggie's were the kind with built-in feet and a hood, and she wore the hood up on her head. They were tiger-striped, and the hood had tiger ears sewn onto it.

"Let's see," said Maggie. "I don't know how to ride a bicycle. I am allergic to shellfish. And I have thirteen pets."

"You have thirteen pets?" Bat said excitedly. "What kinds of pets?"

"Bat," said Janie. "You can't ask questions! That's not how the game works. We have to guess which of the three things is a lie."

"I hope it's true that you have thirteen pets," Bat said to Maggie. She smiled.

"Okay," said Frida. "I think it's true that she's allergic to shellfish. Because that's a weird thing to make up."

Janie nodded, but Israel said, "I think she's lying about not knowing how to ride a bike. Who doesn't know how to ride a bike?"

Then Corinna said, "Well, actually, my mom never learned to ride a bike until she was a grown-up! She just never wanted to when she was a kid."

"That's crazy," Israel said. "I love riding my bike. It's the best! Especially down hills. Up hills, not so much."

Then he and Frida started talking about the really big hill over by the high school, and how hard it was to ride up, and how much fun it was to ride down, until Bat interrupted.

"I think the shellfish thing is the lie," he said, mostly because he really wanted the thirteen-animal thing to be true.

"Okay, who votes shellfish?" Janie asked, and Bat, Israel, Janie, Corinna, and Frida all raised their hand.

"We think the lie is about being allergic to shell-fish," Janie said to Maggie.

She shook her head and grinned. "Nope!" she

said. "I really am allergic to shellfish. They make the inside of my mouth feel all itchy and I break into hives."

Janie tossed a bag of gummies to Maggie, who caught it.

"So what's the lie?" Israel asked.

"It's the animal thing," Maggie admitted. "I don't have thirteen pets . . . I have fourteen!"

"You have fourteen pets?" Bat said. "What kind?"

"We have five chickens," Maggie began, "and two dogs, and seven fish. My brother Jasper has a saltwater tank."

"I want to go next," Bat said.

"Okay," said Janie.

Bat thought for a minute. He didn't like to lie— he really didn't; it made him feel uncomfortable and sort of itchy—but since this was for a game, he wanted to make it a really good lie. When he was ready, he said, "My favorite fruit is grapes, the green ones. When I grow up I'm going to be a fire-fighter. And I have a baby skunk in my room." Then he pointed at Janie and Israel and said, "You guys can't play. Because you know the truths already."

"Okay, Bat," said Janie, rolling her eyes again.

"It's the skunk one," said Maggie. "He just said that because of my pet lie. No one has a skunk for a pet."

Bat tried really hard not to smile.

Corinna said, "Lots of kids want to be a fire-fighter, and everyone likes grapes. I think the skunk thing is the lie, too."

"Skunks are gross," said Frida.

So they all voted that the lie was about having a baby skunk in his room, and Bat, practically bursting with excitement, said, "No! That's the true thing. I really *do* have a baby skunk in my room. His name is Thor."

Then no one cared about which thing was the lie (being a firefighter, of course, because Bat was definitely going to be a veterinarian like his mom when he grew up), and Janie's friends begged him to show them the skunk—even Frida, who had just said that she thought skunks were gross.

"Okay," Bat said. "I'll go get him."

So he went back to his room and scooped up the sleeping kit, blanket and all, and went back into the living room. "You have to be quiet and slow with him," Bat said sternly, "or else he'll be scared. I'll hold him, and you can pet his head."

And then he walked around the circle of kids, showing Thor to each of them. Thor widened his mouth in an adorable yawn, and Janie's friends said, "Oh!" and "Ah!" and told Bat how cute Thor was.

Even Janie took a turn petting Thor's head, and then, because it is what a good friend would do, Bat let Israel carry Thor back to his enclosure.

CHAPTER 18
Best Friends

After Bat put Thor away, Janie got all bossy and told the boys that she and her friends were going to watch a movie that the boys *definitely* wouldn't like, but when Bat asked "What movie?" she wouldn't even say.

"How can you know we won't like it if you won't even let us watch?" Bat said. "What about the time I said I didn't like pigs in a blanket before I'd tried it, and you made me have a bite of yours, and it turned out I really liked it a lot? Do you remember that time?"

"I remember, Bat," Janie said, her mouth in a flat line, "but this is different."

"You boys can watch a movie in my room if you want," Mom offered. Her bedroom was the only one in the house with a TV in it.

But Bat wanted to stay in the living room and ask Maggie more about her pets. What kinds of dogs did she have? How did her brother make sure that the salt water in his fish tank had just the right amount of salt? Did his fish ever try to eat each other? Bat had heard that sometimes fish-tank fish ate each other.

"Come on, Bat," said Israel. "Let's go hang out in your room."

Bat followed, reluctantly.

When they got back to Bat's room, Israel said, "I think your sister was ready to have her friends back to herself."

"What?" said Bat. "But she invited us out there to play a game with them!"

"That's because you need more people for a game to be fun," Israel said. "She doesn't need us to make watching a movie more fun."

Bat thought about that. "Then why didn't she just tell us she was done with us?"

Israel laughed. "Because that's rude!" he said. "Watch." And then he pretended to be Janie:

he put his hands on his hips the way Janie sometimes did and rolled his eyes like Janie and said,
"Bat, I am sick of you and your friend. We don't
need you anymore now that the game is over, so
please go away!" Then he dropped his arms and
grinned. He said, "See? Rude."

"That's a terrible Janie impression," Bat said.
Israel hadn't changed his voice at all, and Janie
always said "Bat" in a long, drawn-out way when
she was annoyed with him, which was often.

Bat looked at Israel. He liked the way Israel's
hair was sort of fluffy, and sort of curly, and sort
of long, but not all the way fluffy or curly or long.
He liked how Israel wore his shirts—loose and
never tucked in—and he liked how Israel almost
always kept his voice low and gentle. There was a
lot to like about Israel.

"You are my best friend," Bat said.

Israel grinned. "Really?" he said. "I didn't think you liked me that much."

"Why would you think that?" Bat asked, bewildered.

"Well," said Israel, "when you are at my house you seem more interested in my dad's truck or my mom's art studio than you are in playing with me."

It was true that on Tuesdays and Thursdays, when Bat went over to Israel's house after school, he used the chance to ask Israel's parents the questions he had. Like, how did a pottery wheel work? (Answer: centrifugal force caused by the spinning of the wheel made the clay move outward from the center.) And, what was the heaviest thing Tom had ever towed with his big black truck? (Answer: a broken-down RV that belonged to one of Tom's friends.)

But those questions didn't mean that Bat didn't think Israel was his best friend. "You have interesting parents," Bat said.

"Thanks, I guess," Israel said.

"You're interesting, too," Bat said. "Even if you're not a professional potter and even though you don't own a big black truck."

This made Israel laugh. "Thanks, Bat," Israel said. "I think you're interesting, too. Even if you didn't have a skunk kit, I'd like you anyway."

"Really?" said Bat. He felt kind of shy and happy at the same time.

"Really," Israel answered.

Bat smiled. Then he said, "Speaking of Thor, do you want to see if we can teach him some tricks?"

"Yes," said Israel. "Yes, I do."

CHAPTER 19
Social Animals

It is not easy to teach a baby skunk to stay, or to sit, or to roll over. But Bat and Israel discovered that Thor could learn one trick: Come.

When Israel pointed Thor in Bat's direction, and Bat said in his sweetest voice, "Thor, baby Thor, come here, baby Thor!" the skunk kit's nose quivered and his feet scuttled clumsily along the ground and his growing black-and-white tail

followed behind him as he made his way across
the distance between the two boys.

"You're the smartest skunk kit in the whole
wide world," Bat cooed to Thor, scooping him up
and kissing his nose, the top of his head, his fuzzy
little paws.

When Thor was too tired to play Come any
more, Bat and Israel fed him a snack of soft bread
and wet dog food and watched as he ate it and

licked his whiskers. Then he retreated to his nest in the kitty carrier, scratched around for a few minutes, and disappeared into silence.

Bat and Israel sat on Bat's railroad rug just outside of Thor's playpen, eating the last snack before bedtime, a bowl of popcorn Mom had brought them. She'd made it in the air popper and had poured melted butter over it and sprinkled salt on top. "It's great how big Thor is getting," Israel said, crunching a mouthful of popcorn. "How long until he'll be ready to release?"

The question made Bat's stomach feel queasy. He dropped his handful of popcorn back into the bowl. "Not for a long time," he said. "He's still barely a toddler. You wouldn't send a toddler out into the cold night all alone, would you?"

"Right," Israel said, "I know not *now*, but, just, how long, do you think? A month? A year? How long do you get to keep him?"

"That's a stupid question," Bat said. He stood up and brushed the popcorn crumbs off his pajamas.

"Why's it stupid?" Israel asked. He was still sitting on the rug, still eating popcorn.

"Because it's stupid!" Bat yelled. Actually, he knew it wasn't a stupid question. It was the same question Bat asked himself over and over, every day. He asked it over and over because he didn't like the answer and kept hoping for a different one. The real answer was that Thor could stay with them until the end of summer, when he would be nearly full-grown and able to forage for food on his own. Then they would have to release him into the wild.

"You know, Bat," Israel said, "sometimes you could be nicer."

How could it be that just a few minutes ago, Bat had been telling Israel that he was Bat's best friend, and now Israel was telling Bat that he wasn't nice?

Everything had felt great and now everything felt terrible.

There was a knock on the door and Mom poked her head in. "Boys," she said, "it's time to brush teeth and climb into bed."

"Okay, Dr. Tam," said Israel, and he got up and headed toward the bathroom.

From the living room, Bat heard the happy laughter of Janie and her friends. It wasn't fair, he thought.

"Mom," Bat said, "Janie is a social butterfly. And I am a social frog."

"Oh, baby." Mom didn't ask what had happened. She just stood next to Bat and put her arms around him, letting him take a step into her hug before she squeezed him tight. "It's late and you're tired," she said. "Things will look better in the morning. Things are always brighter when the sun comes up. For butterflies and for frogs."

CHAPTER 20
Pot Throwing

The sleepover ended at noon the next day, when the last of Janie's friends was picked up by her mother. "See you, Bat," said Frida. "Thank you, Janie. Thank you, Dr. Tam."

The first kid to leave had been Israel. His parents had to pick him up early because they were taking a load of Cora's pottery to the farmer's market to sell, which they did every few months, and Israel had to help.

"It was fun," he had said to Bat before he left, but Bat couldn't tell if that was the truth or not. Bat was still embarrassed about how he had yelled at Israel the night before, but he didn't like to apologize, and anyway Israel shouldn't have kept pushing him about when they would have to release Thor into the wild.

And the next day, a dreary, drizzly sort of day, Israel didn't come to school.

"Maybe he is sick," Mom said. "There's a cold going around." She called Israel's house to find out, and sure enough, she found out that Israel had been under the weather.

"That's a funny expression," Bat said. His voice felt sort of high and tight. "Because you can't really be under the weather. Or over the weather. You can only be in the weather or out of the weather. Don't you think?"

"I think," Mom said, resting one gentle hand

on Bat's shoulder, "that maybe you're still upset about fighting with Israel this weekend. Do you want to talk about it?"

"I want to know what the weather will be like for the rest of the week," Bat said, rolling up onto the balls of his feet.

"You want to know whether the weather will be warm?" Mom said, squeezing Bat's shoulder.

"Yes," said Bat, glad that Mom wasn't going to make him talk about Israel.

Israel was back in school the next day, but he told Bat he didn't feel well enough to do anything together when they got back to his house. He disappeared into his bedroom, leaving Bat in the kitchen with Tom.

"I've got an idea," Tom said. "How about we get our hands dirty?"

Bat was not a big fan of dirty hands. But he didn't feel like saying no to Tom, so he followed him out the back door, across the yard, under a sky dappled with gray clouds, and into Cora's shed.

Cora was there, wrapping a vase in a thick swaddle of newspaper. "This one is on its way to Vermont," she told them. "I just sold it!"

"Great," said Tom. Then, "Want to introduce Bat to the joys of pot throwing?"

For a minute, Bat imagined the three of them picking up the pots from their shelves and throwing them against the walls, hearing them shatter in his imagination.

Cora must have seen the concern on his face, because she quickly said, "Throwing a pot is just another way of saying *making* a pot, on the wheel. It's fun, even if it is sort of sticky and slimy. Do you want to try?"

Actually, Bat would have preferred to go home, or to go to Mom's vet clinic, or even to go back to

Mr. Grayson's classroom. But he couldn't go any of those places, not right now. He had to wait.

So he sat down at the potter's wheel. "Okay," he said.

"Outstanding," said Tom. "First, the clay."

"First, the clay," Cora repeated, and she brought out a large plastic-wrapped cube of clay from under the counter. She peeled back the plastic and picked up a piece of wire with a wooden handle attached to each end. She held the wire against the cube and pulled it through, shaving off a layer of clay. She set it aside and rewrapped the cube in plastic. Then she held out the clay to Bat.

"Squish it into a ball," she said. "Squeeze it hard to get out all the air bubbles."

Bat hesitated, but finally he held out his hand and let Cora place the clay into it. It was cool, almost cold, and damp.

He folded it in his hands and squeezed, forming

a rough ball. His hands turned a dusty gray that dried to white. He squeezed and squeezed.

"Great," said Tom. "Now slam it down hard. Just throw it down, right there, on the wheel."

Bat did. *Thwack* went the clay against the wheel, flattening out in a satisfying way.

"Again," Cora said, so Bat picked up the clay and

re-formed it into a ball. After he threw it a second time, Tom took a turn throwing and shaping it, and then Cora pronounced it ready.

"Okay," said Cora. "Throw it one more time, and this time try to aim right for the center of the wheel."

Bat threw the clay.

"Perfect," Cora said. "Now, Tom will keep the wheel spinning so you don't have to worry about that. I'll help you keep the clay wet. You just cup your hands around the clay, gently but firmly, like you're holding on to something precious. Okay?"

"I'll pretend I'm holding Thor," Bat said. "My skunk kit."

"Great idea," Cora said. "Ready?"

Bat nodded. He cupped his hands around the clay lump. Beside him, Tom stepped gently on the foot pedal, and the wheel began to spin. Cora took a cup of water and poured it in a slow, steady stream over Bat's hands and onto the clay.

"Good," Cora said. "Push the clay down and in. Down and in. Don't worry if it squishes through your fingers! That's fine."

Wet clay oozed out between each of Bat's fingers, and it was a gooey feeling, but not bad. Kind of interesting, actually. Bat watched the clay spinning, spinning, in fast little circles. He watched the clay pushing out between his fingers. He felt almost hypnotized by the sensation of the slippery-wet clay in his hands, spinning, spinning, the challenge of holding it just right in between his fingers and thumbs, not too loosely or it would wobble out of control, not too tightly or the emerging bowl would smoosh in on the side.

But then he could feel the clay beginning to shift off center. It was falling to the side, and he tried to push it back into the center of the wheel, but it seemed like the harder he pushed the worse it got, and then the clay wasn't a ball anymore, it was a weird floppy tube and it was twisting and falling, and then he yelled, "It's breaking!" and flicks of clay splattered his face.

Tom took his foot off the pedal, and the wheel slowed and then stopped. "You did it!" he said, grinning.

"No I didn't," Bat said. "I made a mess."

"Mess is the beginning of art," Cora said. She was smiling, too. "Do you want to try again?"

"Yes," said Bat. "Yes, please."

Before Bat went home, he peeked his head into Israel's room, hoping to tell Israel about how he had learned to make a bowl, about how it wasn't perfectly symmetrical but it was still recognizable as a bowl, and how Cora had called it "creatively catawampus." Maybe he could even say something to let Israel know that he felt bad about their fight.

But Israel was in his bed, his covers pulled up over his chin, his eyes closed. Working with the potter's wheel had made Bat feel so good, and he really wanted to tell Israel all about it. He almost went over to Israel's bed to see if he was really asleep or just resting.

But then Tom called, "Bat! Your mom is here!"

Bat hesitated, looking at the sweaty curls on Israel's forehead. Then, quietly, he backed out of Israel's room, feeling sort of lonely and disappointed that he wouldn't be able to say good-bye.

CHAPTER 21
Scene Stealer

At last, Janie's opening night arrived. Bat felt that it arrived "at last" because it seemed like he'd been hearing Janie talk about it *forever*. In just a few hours, he wouldn't have to hear about how excited Janie was and how nervous Janie was anymore.

"We're leaving in five minutes, Bat!" Mom called from the kitchen. She had already dropped Janie off at the school so that she could get ready. "I get to wear a hoop skirt and makeup and fake eye-lashes," Janie had boasted before she'd left for the show.

That all sounded perfectly terrible to Bat. Clothes should be easy to wear and comfortable, like T-shirts and pants with elastic waists. And the thought of anyone gluing anything to his eyelids made Bat positively twitchy.

Bat looked around his room. He didn't want to go to Janie's play. In the last few weeks, he'd spent so much more time away from home than he was used to that another night out sounded just awful.

And there was little Thor, in his playpen, fin-ished with his dinner and looking up at Bat expectantly. Every night after dinner, Bat had been taking Thor out and working on training him to Come and Stay. They were still working on Stay.

"Oh, little Thor," Bat said to the kit. "You look lonely in there."

Bat felt lonely, too, even though he was about to go to a theater filled with people. Sometimes that was when Bat felt the loneliest of all—in a crowd.

Without really thinking about it, Bat slung Thor's sling around his neck and scooped up the kit, nesting him in place. This time, it was a really tight fit to get Thor into the sling. Bat would have to ask Laurence to make him a bigger one. He grabbed his jacket and put it on over the sling, zipping it up all the way to the top.

"Just settle down and take a nap," Bat

whispered, "and you can come with me to the show."

When Bat came into the kitchen, Mom said, "Are you sure you want to wear your jacket? It's a lovely night."

"I am sure I want to wear my jacket," Bat answered.

Outside of the theater, Bat saw lots of people who had come to see Janie in her play. There was Dad—"Hey, sport! Hi, Valerie," he said to Bat and Bat's mom. There was Laurence—"Bat Boy! Dr. Tam!" he said.

Bat had never seen Laurence wearing regular clothes. He always saw Laurence at the clinic, where Laurence wore blue scrubs. Tonight Laurence was wearing a shirt with buttons and a collar under a sport coat. And his shoes looked like they were made of leather instead of rubber.

"You look . . . different," Bat told Laurence.

Laurence laughed his same laugh, even from inside the different clothes, and that made him seem more like Laurence again.

There was Ezra and his parents, and there was Israel with his mom and dad.

Israel waved at Bat, and Bat waved back, but he felt kind of shy about it. On Thursday, Israel had been all better from his cold, but things still weren't the same between them. They'd shared an awkward snack at Israel's kitchen table before Tom had taken them over to Bat's house to water the skunk garden, and Mom had gotten home early from the clinic.

Finally, it was time to go into Janie's school auditorium, where folding chairs were arranged in rows facing the stage. Bat, his mom, Laurence, and his dad all scooted down a row, not too close to the front but not way in the back, either, and waited for the show to start.

"Bat, baby, do you want to take off your jacket?" Mom whispered as the lights were going dark.

Bat slid the zipper down a little, but then shook his head no. He felt Thor rustle around and then settle back down.

And then the music started and the curtains opened, and the kids started singing and dancing. It took a minute, but then Bat recognized Maggie. She looked different in her Alice costume, a blue dress with a white apron, white tights, and flat black shoes. She looked older than she'd looked at the sleepover, when she'd been wearing those tiger footie pajamas.

But when Janie came on stage dressed as the queen, with a red hoop dress, a giant red crown, and eyelashes that Bat could see from the audience, he didn't recognize her at all until Mom leaned over and whispered, "Look! It's your sister!"

Even then, Bat didn't totally believe that it could be Janie; she looked taller than she looked in regular life, and she moved across the stage like she really was the queen of something.

When she opened her mouth to sing her solo, Bat's mouth opened, too, in surprise.

It *was* Janie! That was the same song she'd been practicing all month, amplified by the microphone she wore taped to her cheek, supported by the music that played along with her, backed up by all the other performers as they danced behind her.

"She's amazing," Bat whispered. Janie's song was so strong and loud and wonderful that Bat leaned forward in his seat.

He had no idea that Janie could be so wonderful. He had no idea that she was so talented and
brave.

He had no idea that—

"Skunk!" yelled a voice in the dark, high-pitched
and loud.

"Skunk!" yelled another voice, and then another,
until the auditorium rattled with yells.

And then it was filled with something worse—
the sharp, acrid stink of a skunk's first spray.

Chairs turned over as the audience rushed
toward the exits. Bat, panicked, eyes stinging from
the odor, dropped to the ground and felt around
desperately for Thor.

Oh! What a mistake it had been to bring the kit!

"Thor!" he cried into the dark. Beside him, his
mom called, "Thor!"

And then Bat heard Dad's voice: "Thor!"

And Laurence: "Thor!"

Someone turned the lights on and Bat spied a black-and-white tail two rows up, sticking out from behind an overturned chair. Quick as he could, Bat scuttled over on his hands and knees and scooped the kit into his arms, cradling him close.

Bat blinked against the sudden light. He looked up. And there, on the stage, arms crossed, crown listing to one side, stood Janie.

CHAPTER 22
No Tomato Juice

"Bat!" It was Israel, in the parking lot. "Is Thor okay?"

Bat nodded, which made the tears brimming in his eyes spill down his cheeks. "Thor is fine," he said. "He's right here." He patted the sling.

"Bat, buddy, I really don't think it was a good idea to bring that thing to your sister's play," Dad said.

"Thor isn't a thing." Only the thought of the frightened kit tucked back into his sling kept Bat from yelling the words.

"Okay, Bat," said Mom in her soothing voice. "Let's go home." She opened the rear door of their station wagon and ushered Bat inside. Janie was already sitting in the car, in the seat next to Bat.

She had changed out of the hoop skirt and crown and back into her regular clothes, but she still had her makeup on, and her arms were still crossed.

She didn't say anything to Bat when he got into the car. She didn't say anything when Mom got into the front seat and started the engine, and she didn't say anything the whole ride home. Not one word about how Thor had sprayed in the middle of her solo, clearing out the auditorium. Not one word about how Bat had ruined the whole play. Nothing.

Bat had wished in the past that Janie would stop talking so much. Right now, though, Bat wished his sister would say something. Anything.

"Keeping that skunk kit was the worst idea ever," Janie said when they got home, before she got out of the car. "I wish Mom had never brought him home."

Anything, Bat thought, except that.

Bat had a terrible night's sleep. It was partially because he still smelled a little bit like skunk spray. Mom had washed his clothes and had given him a mixture of hydrogen peroxide, baking soda, and dish soap to scrub with in the shower, and Bat had washed with it from head to toe, even though Thor hadn't sprayed directly on him. She'd also called everyone she could think of who was at the show and might have gotten sprayed to tell them about the recipe. "It's the only thing that works," she said, over and over again into the phone. "No, tomato juice doesn't really work," she said. And, again and again, Bat heard her say, "I am so sorry this happened. So, so sorry."

But it wasn't really the skunky smell that kept Bat from sleeping.

At the breakfast table, it was obvious that Bat wasn't the only one who had had a poor night's sleep. Janie's eyes were red-rimmed and puffy, and

Mom, too, looked tired, yawing over her steaming mug of coffee.

Janie refused to eat anything at all. "I have no appetite," she insisted, even when Mom offered to make her chocolate chip pancakes.

"At least have a piece of fruit," Mom insisted.

"Half the school was there last night, you know," Janie said to Bat. "Everyone is going to be making jokes all day. Probably for the rest of the year. About my performance stinking."

"Your performance didn't stink," Bat started to say. He wanted to tell Janie that her performance had been wonderful. That because she was so very wonderful, he'd forgotten to keep Thor tightly tucked in. Because she'd been so great, he'd practically forgotten that he was in a theater at all. But before he could say any of this, she shoved back her chair and stood up.

"I might as well go to school and get it over with," she said. She took an apple from the bowl on the table and grabbed her lunch bag from the counter. "See you later, Mom," she said.

She didn't say good-bye to Bat. She didn't even look at him.

Janie and Bat didn't always get along. Bat knew that sometimes Janie thought he was annoying, and that she didn't always love taking care of him. Sometimes she got mad, and sometimes he got mad. But this felt different. This felt huge.

CHAPTER 23
Company

Bat found that he didn't have much of an appetite, either, so after he'd pushed his eggs around his plate for a while, Mom drove him to school. It turned out that everyone there had heard about what had happened at the play, too. From the moment Bat got out of the car, questions followed him:

"Bat, did you really take your skunk to the play?"

"Bat, is it true that the auditorium has to be shut down for a whole *week*?"

"Bat, can you really train a skunk to spray on purpose?"

"Everybody calm down," Mr. Grayson said from the front of the class.

Bat wished he could disappear. He wished he didn't have skin for people to look at or ears for people to talk into.

Mr. Grayson must have assigned something for the class to do because all around the room kids were rifling through their desks and flipping open books.

"Bat," Mr. Grayson said, kneeling beside Bat's desk, "what can I do to help you?"

Bat shook his head. He didn't have any words. He shook his head more and then he shook it harder and harder, and he kept shaking it.

"Bat," said Mr. Grayson, but Bat shook his head

on and on, like the pendulum of a clock, back and forth, left right, left right, left right.

And Mr. Grayson stayed, right there, kneeling next to Bat's desk, his hand on Bat's shoulder.

Finally, Bat felt better. His throat felt normal again, and it didn't bother him so much that he had skin and ears. Mr. Grayson squeezed his shoulder one more time, then stood up. "I think," he said to Bat, "that Babycakes could use some cuddles. Are you the man for the job?"

There in her enclosure was Babycakes, ears flopping, nose twitching. Bat sat cross-legged and held out one of the apple slices Mr. Grayson had given him. He had watched Mr. Grayson take the apple out of his own lunch sack, which he kept in his orange satchel next to his big desk at the front of the room, and cut it up with a pocketknife.

Babycakes hopped over to Bat and sniffed the

apple slice before accepting it. Once she was happily chewing, Bat lifted her up and tucked her into the space between his crossed legs.

Behind him, class went on—they were talking about a book they'd been reading, about a girl with magical powers that allowed her to pause time and fix past mistakes, which at this moment sounded wonderful to Bat, even though he had read the book, too, and knew that every time the girl fixed one mistake, three more popped up in its place.

Bat wondered if new, different mistakes would be better than the mistakes he had made—taking Thor to the play, ruining Janie's big night, and not knowing how to be a better friend to Israel, maybe not being his friend anymore at all.

"Do you want some company?"

Bat looked up. It was Israel.

"I have company," Bat said, petting Babycakes.

Israel sighed. "I know," he said. "I meant *human* company."

"Oh," said Bat. "Yes. Actually, I would like *your* company."

This made Israel smile. He climbed into the enclosure and sat down next to Bat. He leaned over and scratched Babycakes between the ears, just the way she liked.

They sat quietly together for a while. Then Bat said, all at once, "Are you still mad at me?"

"A little," said Israel. "Not really."

"If you're still mad at me," Bat asked, "even a little, then why are you being my company?"

"Because," said Israel, "you're my best friend, right?"

Bat's eyes began to sting like little needle pricks. "Yes," he said, but he looked down at Babycakes's fluffy angora fur and her sideways ears, not up at Israel.

"Best friends need to stick together," Israel said. He reached over and pet Babycakes, his fingers disappearing into her soft white fur.

Then he said, "Bat, I have an idea for how you can apologize to Janie."

CHAPTER 24
Take Two

Apologizing was not something that Bat was very good at. Also, it was something he didn't have very much practice doing. Usually, apologies didn't *do* anything, and that was the problem with them: an apology was just words.

Bat especially hated it when people tried to *force* you to apologize for something. Because no one can make someone sorry, and no one believes an apology that is forced.

Mr. Grayson didn't believe in making people apologize. "I can't make you sorry," he was fond of saying. "Words are cheap." That's something else he was fond of saying. "What we *do* is more important than what we *say*." That was another "Mr. Grayson Special," as he liked to call his favorite sayings.

And Bat agreed with Mr. Grayson. *Doing* something meant more than *saying* something. So if Bat was going to apologize to Janie, it was going to be an active apology.

Lucky for Bat, he had a friend who was very good at doing things. Better than Bat was, Bat admitted to himself. Bat liked to be good at things—he liked to be an expert. And to be an expert, you have to learn from experts. When Bat wanted to learn more about the care and feeding of skunks, he'd gone straight to a world skunk expert, Dr. Jerry Dragoo.

"I'm an expert at apologizing," Israel assured him, "because I'm an expert at making mistakes."

This weekend was an Every-Other Weekend, so Dad picked Bat up after school. Normally they would have picked Janie up next, but Dad told Bat that Janie would be spending the afternoon with one of her friends. The first thing Bat asked Dad, before he even got into Dad's little car, was, "Can you take me over to Israel's house after breakfast tomorrow? He and I have a project we need to work on."

"A school project?" Dad asked.

"No," said Bat. "A secret project."

On Sunday evening at five o'clock, everything was ready. Bat and Israel had set up two rows of chairs in Israel's backyard. Israel's mom had lined the walkway with clay bowls, each filled with water and topped with a floating candle. The night before, Dad had helped Bat find the phone numbers for Frida and Corinna and Maggie, and Bat had called them all.

"I know I messed up your play," he told each of them, "and I want to make it up to Janie. Will you come over to my friend Israel's house at five o'clock on Sunday night?"

Mom was there, with Janie's favorite brownies, just like Bat had asked.

Soon Israel's yard was full of people. Even Laurence came, wearing his blue scrubs again. "Sorry, Bat, I didn't have time to change," he said.

"That's all right," Bat told him. "You look more like yourself this way."

Laurence laughed his wonderful laugh. His laugh was one of Bat's very favorite sounds in the world.

Finally, Bat heard the honk of Dad's car from the front of the house. "Janie's here!" Bat announced, running up the pathway to the front of the yard. His heart beat as if he'd run all the way around the block, and his arms folded into his excited-flapping motion.

Tom went to the front door to let Dad and Janie in, and a minute later he led them out the back door and into the yard.

Janie's eyebrows shot up and her mouth opened in a surprised O as she stepped onto the grass. Bat saw her seeing the people in the two rows of chairs, the glowing, floating candles along the path, and, in front of the garden shed where Israel's mom made her pottery, a little stage they had set up with a curtain hanging as a backdrop, and Mr. Grayson, sitting off to the side with his keyboard, ready to play.

"What is all this?" Janie asked Dad, who was at her side.

"Ask Bat," Dad said, nodding in Bat's direction.

Janie's arms began to fold across her chest again, like she was remembering that she was still mad, but then they loosened and dropped to her sides.

"Bat," she said, walking over to him, "what's going on?"

"I'm sorry I brought Thor to your show and I'm sorry that he sprayed," Bat said. He noticed that Janie was wearing sandals and that she had painted her toenails dark blue. There were little stars painted on the big toes. He talked to the painted-on stars.

"You're a really great singer," Bat said. "Will you sing your solo again? Mr. Grayson can play the music."

For a second that felt like a minute, Janie didn't

say anything. Then she put her hand under Bat's chin and raised up his face so that she could look into his eyes.

Bat didn't love looking into people's eyes, but he knew that Janie really liked to, and he remembered what Mom had told him about how some people learn things about each other from their eyes. So even though it wasn't Bat's favorite thing to do, he stared right into Janie's eyes, which were almost exactly like his own eyes, Bat realized, a brown so dark it was almost black, and shiny.

Maybe Janie saw something in his eyes that let her know that he really was sorry, or maybe she just liked the candles and the stage, because she smiled and gave Bat a hug, which he *did* like, the press of her arms, the smell of her apple shampoo.

"Oh, Bat," she said. "The school is going to redo the play next weekend, after the auditorium has

aired out. But this was really nice of you to set up. And, anyway, the whole thing *was* pretty funny, when you think about it." She dropped her voice to a whisper, just for Bat to hear. "Also, I didn't mean it when I said that I wished Mom had never brought Thor home. I'm sorry I said that." She let him out of the hug and said to the audience, "Hi, everybody. Thank you for coming!"

And then everyone began to clap for Janie—her friends, and Bat's friends, and their family, and Mr. Grayson. And then Janie walked up to the little stage, and she nodded at Mr. Grayson to start playing.

Bat sat down next to Israel, who had saved a seat for him. Then he pulled something out of his pocket to show to Israel. It was the clay skunk Israel had made for him.

"Hey!" Israel whispered. "You're carrying it!

That's so cool!" Bat grinned and rubbed his fingers along the clay lump, memorizing the way the words "From Israel" felt against his thumb. Thor wasn't with him, but Bat felt a sweet warmth in his chest, almost as if the skunk kit was cuddled there.

Janie started to sing, surprising Bat all over again with her strong, clear voice. It was beautiful. The evening was beautiful. The rows of chairs were beautiful. The people in them were beautiful. The floating candles were beautiful. The lump of clay in Bat's hand was beautiful. Right now, the whole world felt giant and open and full of beauty, and Bat was happy.

Acknowledgments

I am grateful for the thoughtful and keen eyes of Corinne Duyvis, the helpful input of real-life skunk expert Dr. Theodore Stankowich, and the careful devotion of this book's first readers, including Rubin Pfeffer, Adah Nuchi, Sasha Kuczynski, and my wonderful editor, Jordan Brown, who loves Bat as much as I do.

Thanks are also due to Charles Santoso, whose beautiful, gentle work illustrating Bat and his world gives the story a new dimension, and the people of Walden Pond Press who champion Bat and his story, especially Debbie Kovacs and Danielle Smith—go, Team Bat!

I especially appreciate my own dear family and my menagerie of pets, from whom I draw inspiration and who always have time to help me brainstorm.

I'm grateful to the teachers, librarians, booksellers, and parents who hand Bat to young readers. Thank you.